# Ella's Sunday Song

Publishing services provided by Krystal Lee Enterprises (KLE Publishing)
Copyright © 2024 by Nicole Franklin All rights reserved.
Please send comments and questions:
Krystal Lee Enterprises
sales@KLEPub.com
770-240-0089 Ext. 1

To Reach the Author:
Web: AuthorNicoleFranklin.com

Printed in the United States of America.
All rights reserved. No part of this book may be reproduced or transmitted in any form or by any means, electronic or mechanical, including photocopying, recording or any information storage and retrieval system without written permission of the publisher except for brief quotations used in reviews, written specifically for inclusion in a newspaper, blog, magazine, or academic paper.
ISBN: 978-1-945066-55-9

# Foreword

Ella's Sunday Song is a children's storybook about the power of the Spiritual "Steal Away" and other Spirituals to inspire thousands and thousands of enslaved people to seek freedom.

Young children will hopefully search for some of the secrets hidden in the words "Steal Away" (code for *quietly slip away*) and "I ain't got long to stay here" (code for *it's time to run*). And in other Spirituals, the use of coding encouraged men, women, and children to do the following:

1. Run to Jesus (code for *run north to freedom*);
2. Be alert for directions and look to the sky for pathways;
3. Watch for *angels* (codes for *guides* and *conductors* with the Underground Railroad).

Spirituals offered multiple strategies, as evidenced in the lyrics of "Wade In the Water" sung to remind escaping persons to trick dogs by wading in rivers and streams to avoid capture.

Read "Ella's Sunday Song" to see how the Spiritual "Steal Away" opens little Ella's heart, mind, and soul to understand the bravery and brilliancy of the ancestors as told by Grandmother Luella.

-Irene Clay Franklin

ELLA can't wait for Sunday. When Ella sings, she can reach all of the high notes...and belt out the really low notes. And this Sunday, she will sing a solo.

Ella practices her song. "Steal Away. Steal Away. Steal Away to Jesus."

Ella looks at her Grandmother, "But you've been here all my life." Grandma says, "I didn't make up the words, Ella."

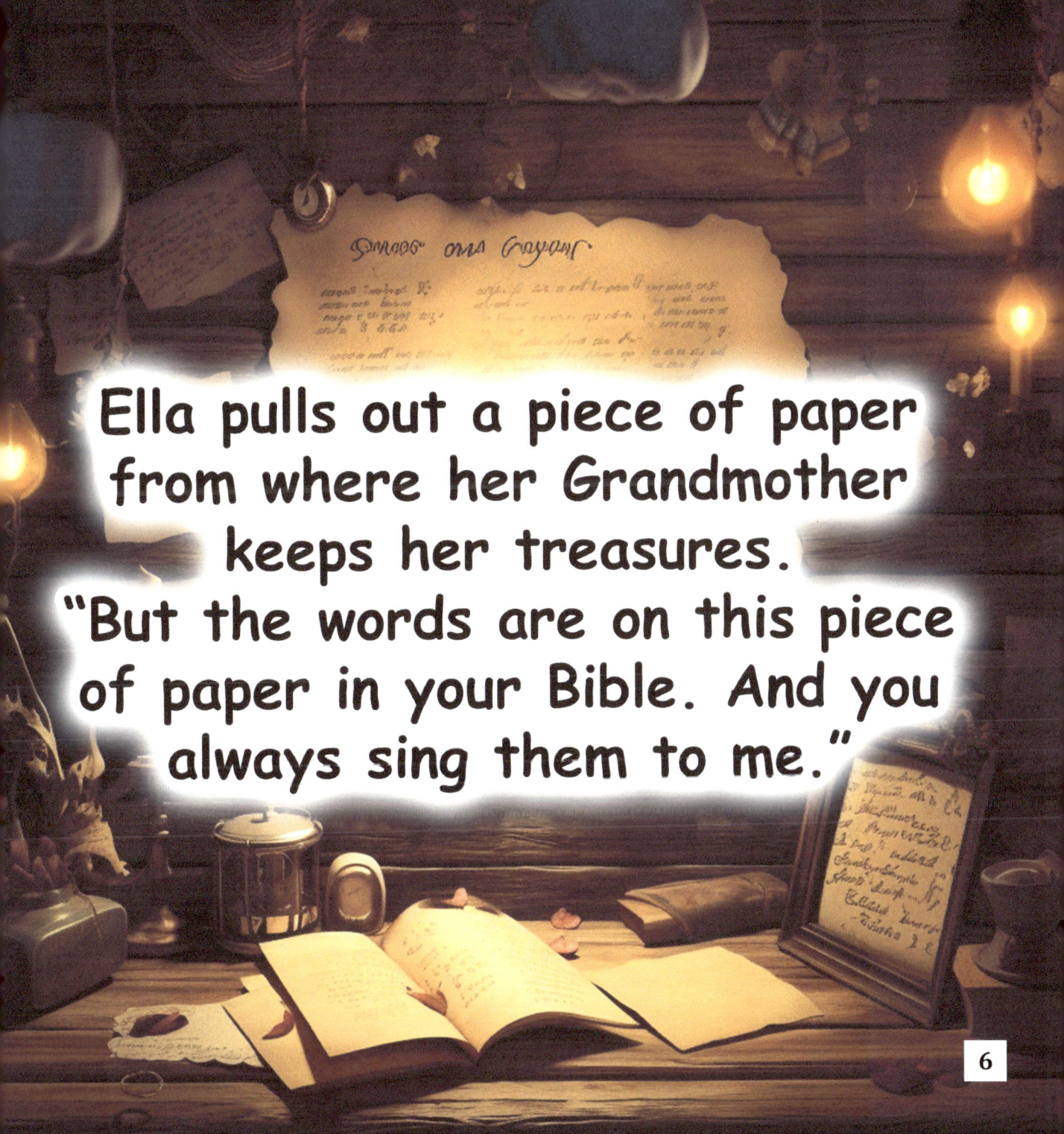

Ella pulls out a piece of paper from where her Grandmother keeps her treasures.
"But the words are on this piece of paper in your Bible. And you always sing them to me."

Grandma Luella says, "Well, I'm glad you've been listening. You'll be singing all the words this Sunday by yourself. Everyone is looking forward to your solo."

Suddenly, Ella hears her friend Franklin playing his trumpet outside. Ella listens and says, "I wish Franklin could play his trumpet this Sunday with me, but I have to sing by myself…" Ella proudly states, "…because – I am the soloist."

Ella thinks for a minute.
Ella says, "When I sing the words, 'Steal Away to Jesus,' Grandma, does Jesus mean a place?"

Ella's Grandmother tells her, "It means you're going to live."

Ella says, "But I heard a lot of the people before us died in slavery."

Grandmother Luella says,
"Yes, our ancestors...our kin."
Ella's Grandmother tells her this story.
"Singing songs is why so many of our ancestors survived. Words led the way to a better place. Did you know your song, 'Steal Away,' holds secret messages, Ella?"

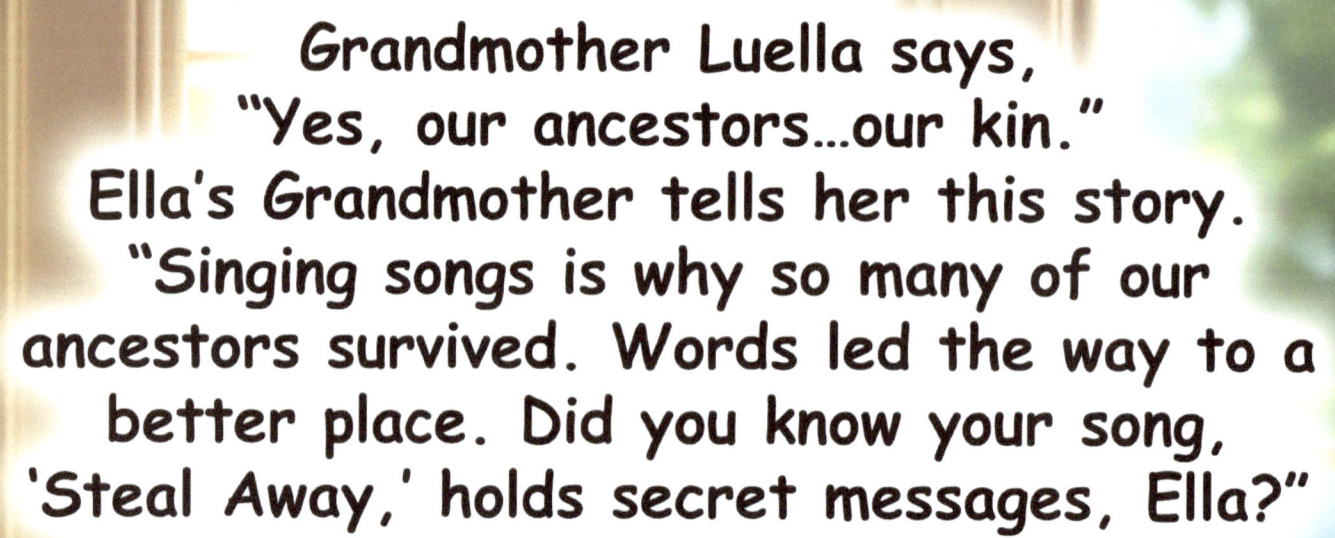

Ella sings, "Steal Away, Steal Away Home. I ain't got long to stay here."
Ella thinks for a minute and says, "What kind of secret messages?"

Church bells ring outside. Ella sings, "It's Noontime!"
Ella knows the church bells are her cue to visit the choir director, three doors down, to practice her song.

Everyone on Ella's neighborhood block knows Ella can sing. As her Grandmother Luella says, "Ella can saaaaang." Ella's walk to her choir director's house is just long enough to practice the first verse of her song.

Ella continues to sing, "The trumpet sounds within my soul." Franklin blows his horn to echo her words. His notes are a perfect fanfare.

Ella waves to him as she looks over her shoulder towards the church, at the dark clouds above the steeple, where the noon bells rang.
"I ain't got long to stay here."

Ella enters the house. "Hi, Ms. Amara. My song for Sunday has a secret. Can you keep a secret?"
Ms. Amara says, "I sure can, Ella."

Ella says, "Steal away to Jesus. Steal away home. After my song, people in the Church will say, Home means our Heavenly Home."
Ms. Amara says, "Well, 'Steal Away' is a spiritual."
Ella says, "But Heaven can mean a place here on Earth. My Grandmother Luella says singing spirituals brought our ancestors a lil' bit of freedom."

A strong breeze blows outside Ms. Amara's window. Ella peers out of the window and continues to reveal the secret. "My song talks about loud sounds. But it doesn't make sense that trumpets can play in a soul. They can be loud like thunder! I think when they sang this song, right before a storm, my ancestors knew it was time to run."

Ms. Amara says, "It was a dangerous run, Ella. They had to escape..."

"...and steal away, and run to their freedom places!" said Ella as she turns away from the window and goes to hug Ms. Amara.

Ms. Amara says, "I gave this song to you, Ella, not just because you're an amazing singer..."

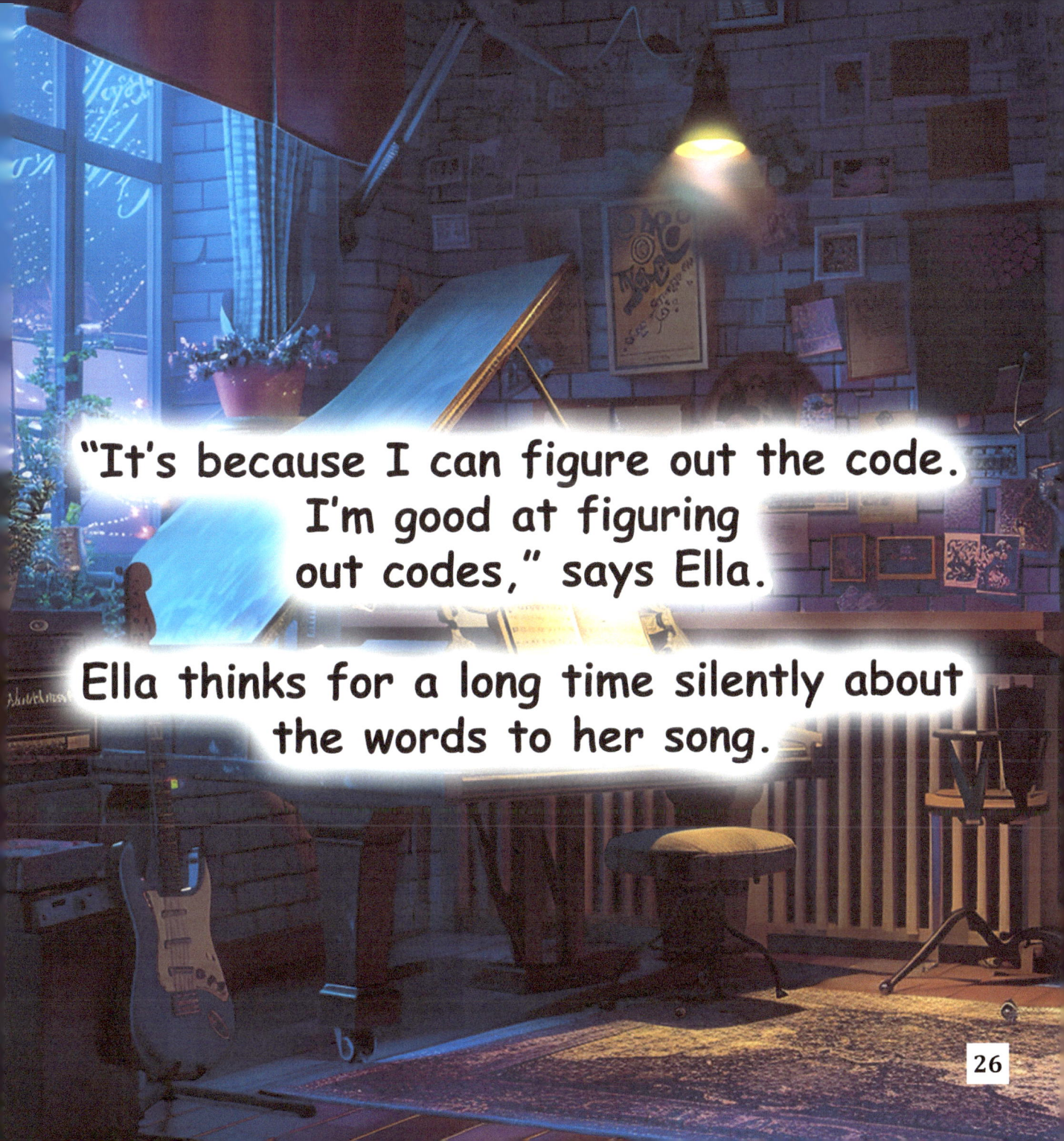

"It's because I can figure out the code. I'm good at figuring out codes," says Ella.

Ella thinks for a long time silently about the words to her song.

Ms. Amara places her hands on the piano keys and says to Ella, "Deep breath."

Ella sings,
"Steal away, steal away,
steal away to Jesus!
Steal away, steal away home,
I ain't got long to stay here."
Ms. Amara plays along on the piano as Ella finishes singing the whole song.

Ms. Amara turns to her young soloist, "Did you hear that?"
Ella looks up and proclaims, "I know."
Ella runs to the door and says, "It's time to go home!"

**Ella's Sunday Song** is a children's picture book introducing the Spiritual, a musical art form that emerged from centuries of enslavement in the United States.

# VOCABULARY WORD LIST

Ancestors
Code
Fanfare
Kin/Kinfolk
Spiritual

# BIBLIOGRAPHY

Guenther, Eileen. "In Their Own Words:  Slave Life and the Power of Spirituals." *MorningStar Music Publishers; 1st edition*, June 1, 2016, pp 124-125, 380, 358.

Higginson, Thomas Wentworth. "Army Life in a Black Regiment." *Boston: Fields, Osgood, & Co*, 1870.

Johnson, James Weldon and J. Rosamund Johnson. "The Book of American Negro Spirituals." *Kessinger Publishing*, LLC, 2010.

Lovell, John. "Black Song:  The Forge and the Flame:  The Story of How the Afro-American Spiritual Was Hammered Out." *Macmillan*, 1972.

Lovell, Jr. John. "The Social Implications of the Negro Spiritual." *The Journal of Negro Education*, vol. 8, no. 4, October, 1939, pp 634-643.

Johnson, Thomas A. "Spirituals, Reflecting New Attitude, Regain Popularity." *The New York Times, September* 30, 1971.

# Get Published with KLE Publishing!

If you need a ghostwriter, editor, or want to publish a book visit KLEPub.com or call 770-240-0089 Ext. 1

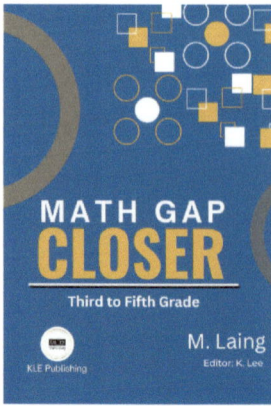

Milton Keynes UK
Ingram Content Group UK Ltd.
UKHW050754151024
449707UK00020B/7

*9 781945 066559*